POEMS

Also by Ron Rash

POEMS

{ NEW AND SELECTED }

RON RASH

An Imprint of HarperCollins*Publishers*

OCT '16

HarperCollins books may be purchased for educational, business, or sales promotional use. For information, please e-mail the Special Markets Department at SPsales@harpercollins.com.

FIRST EDITION

Designed by Suet Yee Chong

Library of Congress Cataloging-in-Publication Data has been applied for.

ISBN 978-0-06-243550-7

16 17 18 19 20   OV/RRD   10 9 8 7 6 5 4 3 2 1

For family

"I had my existence. I was there.
Me in place and the place in me."

—Seamus Heaney, "A Herbal"

Contents

EUREKA MILL

WAKING

NEW POEMS

RESOLUTION

The surge and clatter of whitewater conceals
how shallow underneath is, how quickly gone.
Leave that noise behind. Come here
where the water is slow, and clear.
Watch the crawfish prance across the sand,
the mica flash, the sculpin blend with stone.
It's all beyond your reach though it appears
as near and known as your outstretched hand.

RAISING
THE DEAD

LAST SERVICE

Though cranes and bulldozers came,
yanked free marble and creek stones
like loose teeth, and then shovels
unearthed coffins and Christ's
stained glass face no longer paned
windows but like the steeple,
piano, bell, and hymnals
followed that rolling graveyard
over the quick-dying streams,
the soon obsolete bridges—
they still congregated there,
wading then crossing in boats
those last Sunday nights, their farms
already lost in the lake,
nothing but that brief island
left of their world as they lit
the church with candles and sang
from memory deep as water
old hymns of resurrection
before leaving that high ground
where the dead had once risen.

UNDER JOCASSEE

One summer morning when
the sky is blue and deep
as the middle of the lake,
rent a boat and shadow
Jocassee's western shoreline
until you reach the cove that
once was the Horsepasture River.
Now bow your head and soon
you'll see as through a mirror
not a river but a road
flowing underneath you.
Follow that road into
the deeper water where
you'll pass a family graveyard,
then a house and barn.
All that's changed is time,
so cut the motor and drift
back sixty years and remember
a woman who lived in that house,
remember an August morning
as she walks from the barn,
the milking done, a woman
singing only to herself,
no children yet, her husband
distant in the field.
Suddenly she shivers,
something dark has come
over her although

no cloud shades the sun.
She's no longer singing.
She believes someone
has crossed her grave, although
she will go to her grave,
a grave you've just passed over,
wondering why she looked up.

TAKING DOWN THE LINES

They tore the telephone lines
from the valley like unhealed
stitches, poles and wires hauled off
through which voices had once flowed
across Jocassee like freshets
crisscrossing, running backward
into far coves where one phone
might be shared by five families.
In those lines was sediment
of births and sickness, deaths,
love vows and threats, all passed on
mouth to mouth, vital as breath
before silenced in the lake's
currents of lost connections.

FALL CREEK

As though shedding an old skin,
Fall Creek slips free from fall's weight,
clots of leaves blackening snags,
back of pool where years ago
local lore claims clothes were shed
by a man and woman wed
less than a month, who let hoe
and plow handle slip from hands,
left rows half done, crossed dark waves
of bottomland to lie on
a bed of ferns, make a child,
and all the while the woman
stretching both arms behind her
over the bank, hands swaying
wrist-deep in current—perhaps
some old wives' tale, water's pulse
pulsing what seed might be sown,
or just her need to let go
the world awhile, let the creek
wash away every burden
her life had carried so far,
open a room for this new
becoming as her body
flowed around her man like water.

SHEE-SHOW

Shortia galacifolia, commonly known as Oconee Bells

Michaux called it Shortia
for a London friend, a word
read more than spoken because
white settlers let place and shape
inspire a prettier name,
a rich feel of syllables
rung off the tongue, merging two
cultures for once without blood,
though now so long after those
namegivers have vanished like
what was here, I remember
the Cherokee word, the smooth
surface of its cadence, how
it promised coming water.

DEEP WATER

The night smooths out its black tarp,
tacks it to the sky with stars.
Lake waves slap the bank, define
a shoreline as one man casts
his seine into the unseen,
lifts the net's pale bloom, and spills
of threadfin fill the live well.
Soon that squared pool of water
flickers as if a mirror,
surfaces memory of when
this deep water was a sky.

IN DISMAL GORGE

The lost can stay lost down here,
in laurel slicks, false-pathed caves.
Too much too soon disappears.

On creek banks clearings appear,
once homesteads. Nothing remains.
The lost can stay lost down here,

like Tom Clark's child, our worst fears
confirmed as we searched in vain.
Too much too soon disappears.

How often this is made clear
where cliff-shadows pall our days.
The lost can stay lost down here,

lives slip away like water.
We fill our Bibles with names.
The lost can stay lost down here.
Too much too soon disappears.

BLACK-EYED SUSANS

The hay was belt-buckle high
when rain let up, three days' sun
baked stalks dry, and by midday
all but the far pasture mowed,
raked into windrows, above
June sky still blue as I drove
my tractor up on the ridge
to the far pasture where strands
of sagging barbed wire marked where
my land stopped, church land began,
knowing I'd find some grave-gift,
flowers, flag, styrofoam cross
blown on my land, and so first
walked the boundary, made sure what
belonged on the other side
got returned, soon enough saw
black-eyed Susans, the same kind
planted in my yard, a note
tight-folded tied to a bow.
Always was all that it said,
which said enough for I knew
what grave that note belonged to,
and knew as well who wrote it,
he and her married three months
when he died, now always young,
always their love in first bloom,
too new to life to know life
was no honeymoon. Instead,

she learned that lesson with me
over three decades, what fires
our flesh sparked too soon put out
by time and just surviving,
and learned why old folks called it
getting hitched, because like mules
so much of life was one row
you never saw the end of,
and always he was close by,
under a stone you could see
from the porch, wedding picture
she kept hid in her drawer,
his black-and-white flashbulb grin
grinning at me like he knew
he'd made me more of a ghost
to her than he'd ever be.
There at that moment—that word
in my hand, his grave so close,
if I'd had a shovel near
I'd have dug him up right then,
shown her the bones, made her see
what the truth was, for memory
is always the easiest
thing to love, to keep alive
in the heart. After awhile
I laid the note and bouquet
where they belonged, never spoke
a word about it to her

then or ever, even when
she was dying, calling his
name with her last words. Sometimes
on a Sunday afternoon
I'll cross the pasture, make sure
her stone's not starting to lean,
if it's early summer bring
black-eyed susans for her grave,
leave a few on his as well,
for soon enough we'll all be
sleeping together, beyond
all things that ever mattered.

WHIPPOORWILL

The night Silas Broughton died
neighbors at his bedside heard
a dirge rising from high limbs
in the nearby woods, and thought
come dawn the whippoorwill's song
would end, one life given wing
requiem enough—were wrong,
for still it called as dusk filled
Lost Cove again and Bill Cole
answered, caught in his field, mouth
open as though to reply,
so men gathered, brought with them
flintlocks and lanterns, then walked
into those woods, searching for
death's composer, and returned
at first light, their faces lined
with sudden furrows as though
ten years had drained from their lives
in just one night, and not one
would say what was seen or heard,
or why each wore a feather
pressed to the pulse of his wrist.

SHELTON LAUREL

Sister, I have come to understand
the world will have its way with us despite
what we might wish, or once believed. Last week
I watched our neighbors die like snakes. Gut-shot,
then hacked with hoes until their moaning ceased.
Shelton's youngest son was one of them,
alive thirteen years. His eyes met mine,
but like his father and brothers he didn't speak.
It was past words by then but still I thought
of all the times the five of us had shared
a hunting camp, spun lies at Allen's Store,
better times before we let this war
settle like a vulture in these hills,
a vulture never sated. Though I aimed
my rifle to the right it didn't matter,
others found the mark with lead or hoe.
And when it ended the sun burned in the sky
like any other day. The French Broad still
flowed on down to Marshall. In the trees
fox squirrels chattered, wrens still sang their song.
By noon the snow had turned from white to red.
Our sergeant danced like a dervish on the grave,
vowed he'd push them deeper into hell.
And I was there, dear sister, I was there,
and still feel I am there although I hide
miles away, deep inside this cavern
and write this letter with what light is left
in one last stub of candle, light enough

to get this letter written, bring to you,
leave it by your pillow while you sleep,
then make my way back here where I will stay.
A branch runs through this cavern, in it trout
whose eyes are blind from years of too much dark.
I envy them for all they haven't seen,
and maybe with enough time I might too
cease to see these things I tell you of,
that drape upon my soul like heavy shackles,
and then return to you, resume a life
stilled like the hands of a broken pocket watch
beside a stream bank deep in Shelton Laurel.

WOLF LAUREL

Tree branches ice-shackled, ground
hard as an anvil, three sons
and a father leave the blaze
huddled around all morning,
wade snow two miles where they cross
Wolf Laurel Creek, poke rifles
in rock holes, cliff leans hoping
to quarry what's killed five sheep,
but no den found as the ridge
sips away the gray last light
of winter solstice, and they
head back toward home, the trail
falling in blur-dark and then
the father falls too, eyes locked,
wrist unpulsed, the sons without
lantern, enough lingering light,
know they must leave him or risk
all of them lost, know what waits
for death in this place, so break
a hole in Wolf Laurel's ice,
come back at first light to find
the creek's scab of cold covered
with snow-drift, circling paw prints
brushed away that sons might see
a father's face staring through
the ice as through a mirror.

SPECKLED TROUT

Water-flesh gleamed like mica:
orange fins, red flankspots, a char
shy as ginseng, found only
in spring-flow gaps, the thin clear
of faraway creeks no map
could name. My cousin showed me
those hidden places. I loved
how we found them, the way we
followed no trail, just stream-sound
tangled in rhododendron,
to where slow water opened
a hole to slip a line in,
and lift as from a well bright
shadows of another world,
held in my hand, their color
already starting to fade.

IN THE BARN

The tin roof folded its wings
above my cousin and me
that day the barn mouth darkened,
swallowed its green tongue before
we filled the last stall with straw.
Thunder lumbered up the gorge,
then a sound like berries dropped
in a pail as tin and wood
creaked and wept, afternoon fell
toward an early night, the last
swallow settled in its nest.
We settled as well, let straw
pillow our heads as rain tucked
its loud hush tighter around us.
My cousin lay on his back,
eyes closed, hands on chest as though
already getting ready
for a wake eight years away.

BARN BURNING: 1967

What was left cast no shadow
but was shadow: a black square
of absence laid like a quilt
on the pasture, not even
smoke left by first light, although
still lingering in the air
like a bitter aftertaste,
tobacco burned too early.
A photograph snapped that day
soon became a talisman,
as if the camera captured
flame forever on that farm,
and when they'd weathered that hard
mountain winter something more—
proof that disaster might be
framed by time to fit inside
rows of happier events.
Whenever the Bible-thick
album sprawled its black-and-white
backward-turning calendar
across the kitchen table,
my uncle would see himself
standing alone in the past,
shoulders hunched, eyes dark and cold
as the ashes at his feet.
A man who gets through a time
mean as that need not have fears
of something worse, he would say.
He said that for seven years.

WORK, FOR THE NIGHT IS COMING

The tobacco leaves blacken,
root deeper in dark but he
will not follow his father
from the field, not until this
end row is finished with what
light windows from the farmhouse,
where supper cools on the stove,
death-clothes scarecrow a bedpost
as the clock hands spread like wings,
widen this moment he tops
his last plant, becomes a part
of the night before he folds
his barlow knife and walks back
up the row, fingers brushing
the future's gold-ripening—
curing tongues of burley hung
from barn rafters, the harvest
his father will reap alone.

THE DEBT

We want him to have the best,
they told Barney Hampton as
he led them to a room where
coffins lay open on shelves
like traps waiting to be sprung,
but because he'd always been
an honest man, and because
he knew how little cabbage
and tobacco brought even
in good years, Barney Hampton
passed copper, stainless steel, stopped
where he could make his pitch for
wood's varnished solidity,
but my uncle and aunt said
what they'd said before, then spent
half a decade stooped in fields
so each fall one more ticket
in the coupon book might be
torn out to pay for what they'd
sown deeper than any seed.

WATAUGA COUNTY: 1974

Cold rain, fog thick as gravestone,
six outstretched hands, one hand mine
as I stand with older kin,
await the undertaker's
tight-lipped nod before I lift
what is left, a body more
light than I had imagined,
so light the casket glides like
a boat on currents of white,
as though what is held holds me
above the earth-door he must
enter alone, the right hand
I feared might not raise him now
not wanting to let him down.

BURNING THE FIELD

My uncle lights the rag fuse
doused with diesel fuel and heaves,
bottle arcing like a flare
before it shatters on ground
between us, flame-spill spreading
like bright roots from middlefield
to the firebreak banks harrowed
that dawn, the banks we vigil
that no spark leap that orange weave
and waver squared in five acres
like a live quilt dying quick
as flame withers; then a gray
smolder like fog rising off
a river, what I walk through
to join my uncle, and now
three decades later wonder
what he saw that afternoon
coming from the other side,
smoke-wreathed, wearing a jacket
passed on, familiar.

AT REID HARTLEY'S JUNKYARD

To enter we find the gap
between barbed wire and briars,
pass the German shepherd chained
to an axle, cross the ditch
of oil black as a tar pit,
my aunt compelled to come here
on a Sunday after church,
asking me when her husband
refused to search this island
reefed with past catastrophes.
We make our way to the heart
of the junkyard, cling of rust
and beggarlice on our clothes,
bumpers hot as a skillet
as we squeeze between car husks
to find in this forever
stilled traffic one Ford pickup,
tires stripped, radio yanked out,
driver's door open. My aunt
gets in, stares through glass her son
looked through the last time he knew
the world, as though believing
like others who come here she
might see something to carry
from this wreckage, as I will
when I look past my aunt's ruined
Sunday dress, torn stockings, find
her right foot pressed to the brake.

SPEAR POINT

No time to exchange one set
of grave clothes for another,
so my cousin rests his back
on a tree trunk, shovel laid
on his lap like a rifle,
as though to guard the hole he,
three other men have opened,
waits there while we fill the pews,
sing and pray inside, and still
by the tree as pallbearers
bring from the church what brings us
through this gate where lambs pasture
under the gaze of angels.
My kinsman does not join
our huddle across the rows
where we soil our hands, begin
what he will finish. Only
when the preacher says amen
does he let go the shovel,
make his way through that acre
of granite stubbed like clearcut,
offer me words, then what weights
his blistered palm—a spear point
lifted from my father's grave.

KEPHART IN THE SMOKIES

The morning woods smolder with fog,
the damp, black leaves slick underfoot.
Horace Kephart follows the prong
that pools and falls in Clingman's shadow,

merges soon with Hazel Creek,
loses altitude and then
becomes the Little Tennessee
to flow against the continent,

toward the nation's center where
he's left six children and a wife,
mapped and compassed his way to here,
found this place to lose himself.

Hungover, cotton-mouthed, he pauses,
his hands like prayer to hold the water.
Trembling its cold against his teeth,
he wishes it were something stronger.

BARBED WIRE

New strung, it sparks a live wire
when sun hits right, and can be
thumbed like guitar string, its tune
pure country twang, but given
enough time rain rusts metal,
fence posts wobble like loose teeth,
barbed wire burrows in laurel
and goldenrod before found
by fishermen or hunters.
As I found out once, deep in
the Smokies when something latched
to my calf—coil of old strands
not quite elemented back
into ground ore, and though I searched
no chimney-spill or hearthstone,
no sign but rusty fence-thorns
of one whose hammer tapped out
a claim on this land traveling
through bright lines from post to post,
traveling time to a moment
one man's tenuous hold on
the earth snagged like a memory
surfaced long after, time-dulled,
but still able to draw blood.

THE SEARCH

What hope we had had died by afternoon.
We should have given up, gone home to eat,
left her in the woods. November frost
would keep her well enough till morning came.
The dead have all the time in the world. Besides
she wasn't our kin. She wasn't even white.
Her and her old man had moved up here
twelve years ago. We didn't know from where.
They never told us. They kept to themselves,
farming a hollow far up Painter Creek,
the only colored we had ever known.

Though there'd been times we helped each other out,
racing rain to get hay in a loft,
finding a cow, building a barn or shed,
the things all farmers do to get along.
So he'd come to us when she wandered off
just like she'd done before, except before
he'd always found her, usually at the creek,
or standing in the fields still as a scarecrow.
She'd got so old she was lost inside her mind,
and wasn't going to get home by herself,
so we left our wives, our after-supper fire.

We didn't find her either that first night
our lanterns lighted up the mountainside,
our voices hoarsened—just her name replied.
At dawn most left, went home to sleep or work.

Four of us decided to stay on.
We took Ezekiel, that was his name,
back to the cabin. The women fixed a meal.
He wanted to go but would only slow us down,
so left behind, his face cupped in his hands,
while we searched until the sun was just a hint
behind Whiteside Mountain as we climbed
up Wildhog Ridge, the one place left to look.

We buttoned up our coats and lit the wicks,
swore we'd only search another hour,
swore that several times before we found her,
back against a tree like she'd been waiting.
A harvest moon broke through a patch of clouds.
We raised her in its light and lantern light,
and looked into a face the frost had burned
as white as dogwood blossoms in the spring.
A soft breeze stirred the leaves and then lay down,
the way a weary hound settles to sleep.
It was so quiet. No one seemed to breathe.

Josh Burton held her first, cradled her
against his chest, stumbled down the ridge.
We all took our turn. The women did the rest,
bathed and dressed her, staying through the night.
We left to get some sleep, not saying much,
thinking of cows to milk, horses to feed.
We'd done all we could. We got her home.

BRIGHTLEAF

A path once smoothed this creek edge—
limb cuts, uproot, laurel slash,
passage enough to get corn,
tobacco to Boone, though now
the way is blazed by water
I have rockstepped and waded
into a gorge that narrows
like a book slowly closing,
what sunfall cliff-snagged, leaf-seined,
a place named for what it was:
Dismal, Shut In, where I find
family lore confirmed, a squared
plot of slant land, full acre
of white petals surrounding
chimney stub once a homestead.
Here a bride planted hundreds
of dogwoods, so coming springs
branches flared with white blossoms,
waking an orchard of light
against that bleak narrative
of place name, a life scratched out
on ground as much rock as dirt.
Decades passed as she raised what
might look from distant summit
like a white flag unfurled, though
anything but surrender.

AT LEICESTER CEMETERY

Six feet below our feet the dead
will not argue or confirm
this ancestral gossip.
Pure Cherokee, my cousin says,
but Baptist so no one cared.
And what of this one? I ask,
pointing to his closest kin.
*He killed a man, then schemed
to marry the dead man's widow.*
Scandal has weathered to dust
as we acknowledge his rashness
with a smile, move to another plot,
just a first name, the rest
time-swept from the creek rock.
Lost, my cousin says. *I can't
find her in county records
or family Bibles. It's like
she never lived.* We walk back,
pass again men with shovels
who finish what has brought
us back to this high country.
You can see forever from here,
my cousin says. We look west,
the mountains leveling out
becoming east Tennessee
before they rise again, distant
against an even more distant sky.

MADISON COUNTY, JUNE 1999

Where North Carolina locks
like a final puzzle piece
into eastern Tennessee,
old songs of salvation rise
through static on Sunday night
in this mountain county where
my name echoes on gravestones
time dimmed as the evening
a kinsman held fire, let it lick
his palm like a pet before
he raised that hand so we might
see providence as his tongue
forged a new language bellowed
in a pentecostal blaze.
That is all I remember:
an unburned hand, those strange words,
what came before or after
on that long-ago Sunday
dark as beyond the headlights
as I practice smaller acts
of faith on hill crests, blind curves,
and though my life lies elsewhere
some whisper inside urges
another destination,
as if that unburned hand were
raised in welcome, still might lead
me to another state marked

by no human boundary,
where my inarticulate
heart might finally find voice
in words cured by fire, water.

THE WOLVES IN THE ASHEVILLE ZOO

Fog grazing among the trees,
and they herd with it, become
whispers of movement until
one bares its throat, then silence
as though pausing for answer
from cliff cave or laurel den
vacant twelve decades—and I
pause too, imagine the first
of my name in this county,
rock and wood raised on a ridge,
wind swaying the boards like waves
as if still inside the ship
sailing from land where wolfpacks
vanished far back as fire-drakes,
denned in blood-memory until
given voice one mountain night
as oak slats rattle like bones,
the hearth's last log cools to ash
gray as his eyes as he pokes
charwood for some nub of light.

THE WATCH

Almost like a scythe, the sweep
of mesh through creek-pool, that slow
harvest of dace and crayfish,
the homemade seine held between
my brother and me, worked deep
in each undercut, sinkers
scraping white sand like a rake,
and this morning a subtle
bowing, then give, bringing up
a gold watch three decades dropped
from our grandfather's pocket,
lost in his field, freshet-swept
to this pool some longback spring.
My knife blade pries open time
like a clam, water spilling
out lost hours, and though I try
with shake and stem wind to rouse,
the hands do not move, remain
at six-thirty, one placed on
the other like dead man's hands.

BARTRAM LEAVES JOCASSEE

So easy to believe he
sensed the lake's coming that day
he climbed Oconee Mountain,
cast a last look back before
descending into Georgia:
The mountainous wilderness
appearing regularly,
undulating as the great
ocean after a tempest.

It's called Station Mountain now,
the place he stood, where I stand,
look back as well, and because
history is sometimes more
than irony, imagine
this restless Quaker followed
the land's slow falling away
until distance disappeared,
and he glimpsed something beyond
what even time could fathom.

CAROLINA PARAKEET

Though once plentiful enough
to pulse an acre field, green
a blue sky, they were soon gone,
whole flocks slaughtered in a day,
though before forever lost
found last here, in these mountains
so sparsely settled a man
late as 1900 might
look up from new-broken land
and glimpse that bright vanishing.

THE VANQUISHED

Even two centuries gone
their absence lingered—black hair
dazzling down a woman's back
like rain, a man's high cheekbones,
a few last names, no field plowed
without bringing to surface
pottery and arrowheads,
bone-shards that spilled across rows
like kindling, a once-presence
keen as the light of dead stars.

A HOMESTEAD ON THE HORSEPASTURE

Those last days he stayed to watch
water tug his farm under
one row at a time, so slow
his eyes snagged no memory
of what was lost, no moment
he could say *I saw it end.*
When little else showed but what
his own hands had raised he soaked
house and barn with kerosene,
shattered a lantern, and as
it burned the taste of ashes
filled his mouth until nothing
remained but what he'd corbeled
out of creek stone he would leave
for the water to reclaim.

BOTTOMLAND

No corn summered green and tall
across Cane Creek's bottomland
that last August. What rose there
was the lake's slow becoming,
though scarecrows stayed like totems
giving loss human measure
each day their stakes sank deeper
like faultless divining rods,
and when October's orange
harvest moon blossomed they stalked
those vanished fields, raised arms spread
like those of the forsaken.

TREMOR

Weight of water was what caused
cups to shiver in cupboards,
cows to pause, Duke Power claimed,
but those who once lived there
thought otherwise, spoke of lives
so rooted in this place some
of their presence yet lingered:
breeze of sickle combing wheat,
stir of hearth-kettle, the tread
of mule across broken ground,
long-ago movements breaking
across time like a fault line.

ANALEPSIS

Fishermen have heard it years,
a wailing from deep water
nights the wind settles, the moon
trembles on the lake as if
light not falling but rising,
as if some things cannot be
forever hidden but must
surface—as believers claim
who remember two creek stones
that marked a life's shallow length,
name and date weathered away,
no other graves, as if that
one grief was enough to fill
a whole meadow, forgotten
those days the other dead rose
cradled in live arms before
returned to earth. So on nights
a wet moon rises it wakes
this child who cries to be held,
gives voice to the underneath
of water, the lost unnamed
dawn-calmed by the dam's pale hand.

THE DAY THE GATES CLOSED

We lose so much in this life.
Shouldn't some things stay, she said,
but it was already gone,
no human sound, the poplars
and oaks cut down so even
the wind had nothing to rub
a whisper from, just silence
rising over a valley
deep and wide as a glacier.

BEYOND THE DOCK

Some stars, quarter slice of moon,
but mainly dark, as the dock
creaks and sways like a cradle.
I lie down, shoulder to wood,
cheek on my arm, my ear close
to the rough boards and I hear
lake waves slosh against clay banks,
low whisper of white oak leaves.
Soon something else, boat motor
purling closer, then shut off,
drifting the deeper water
somewhere out beyond this dock
where my ear leans to the wood
as to a door while a man
and woman convey no words,
only whispered urgency,
then an image when match-flare
sparks a lantern, making more
dark than all else a female
silhouette, the outstretched palm
letting something slip free, then
the hand spread to the lantern
like a magician proving
the coin is gone before
flame sifts from globe-glass like sand,
expires as the motor coughs,
and they leave, leaving some small

piece of two lives that needed
to fall forever away
in a reservoir so vast
it could bury a valley.

THE MEN WHO RAISED THE DEAD

If they had hair it was gray,
the backs of their hands wormy
currents of blue veins, old men
the undertaker believed
had already lost too much
to the earth to be bothered
by what they found, didn't find,
brought there that May afternoon
dogwood trees bloomed like white wreaths
across Jocassee's valley.

They took their time, sought the shade
when they tired, let cigarettes
and silence fill the minutes
until the undertaker
nodded at his watch, and they
worked again, the only sound
the rasp and suck of shovels
as they settled deeper in graves
twice-dug, sounding for the thud
of struck wood not always found—
sometimes something other, silk
scarf or tie, buckle, button
nestled in some darker earth,
enough to give a name to.

One quit before they were done,
lay down as if death were now
too close to resist, and so
another stepped in his grave,
finished up, but not before
they shut his eyes, laid him with
all the others to be saved
if not from death, from water.

AMONG
THE
BELIEVERS

ON THE BORDER

Today it's still hard country,
bare hills, dark valleys, gray juts
of stone against gray sky. Here
men argued map lines with blood,

raised death like a seed crop when
their hearts became their landscape,
as did their acts. One winter
after days of murders, rapes,

burned homesteads, ransacked churches,
a band of reivers turned back
north to the last wide water
before the border, their backs

laden with golden crosses,
chalices that dragged them down
halfway across and they drowned
in a river called Eden.

PLOWING ON MOONLIGHT

I rose with the moon, left the drowsy sheets,
my nine months wife singing in her sleep,
left boots on the floor, overalls and hat
scarecrowing a bedpost so I could plant
my seeds with just a plow between
the earth and me, my pale feet deep
in the ridged wake where I labored,
gripped the handles like a divining rod,
my eyes closed to the few stars out.
All night I plowed, beard budded by frost,
chest nippled, my breath blooming white,
and felt in me the sway of the sea,
rain's fall and soak, the taproot's thrust,
the cicada's winged resurrection.
I opened my eyes to dawnlight,
left my field and lay with my wife,
warming as I pressed against her body,
my hand listening to her waxing belly.

THE CORPSE BIRD

Bed-sick she heard the bird's call
fall soft as a pall that night
quilts tightened around her throat,
her gray eyes narrowed, their light
gone as she saw what she'd heard
waiting for her in the tree
cut down at daybreak by kin
to make the coffin, bury
that wood around her so death
might find one less place to perch.

MADISON COUNTY: 1864

No civil war could be fought
where bloodlines and creeks named sides,
ancestral grudges freed
an intimate politics
of atrocity, so men
authored new testaments from
Jehovah's old laws when they
raised enemies toward heaven,
offerings to be found years
later in hollows and glens,
dangling bones like drawn buckets
above a well, if cut down
left on the ground where they fell,
food for wild hogs. Once a hand
came waving out of the woods
held in a hound's yellow growl,
and down in Shelton Laurel
Widow Franklin told her sons
If you die, die like a dog,
your teeth in somebody's throat.

ON THE WATAUGA

On the bank of a river
he saw a tall tree, one half
crimson fire from root to crown,
the other half green with leaves.
All night the firelight colored
the river red as a wound.
A full moon loomed as he walked
into the waist-deep water,
bathed and tugged by a current
flickering like a cold flame
until the stars dimmed like sparks,
the tall tree's heat lit the sun,
and he staggered to the shore
white-eyed, blinded by Godlight.

BEFORE

Before clock hands showed the time
time ceased, and looking glasses
were veiled as if they still held
familiar faces, in those
last moments when breath shallowed
like a wellspring running dry,
God-words quickened, only then
the dying left death-beds borne
on the arms of the gathered,
lowered to the floor so they
might press close, as though a door
through which to listen and know
the earth's old secrets before
it opened, and they entered.

THE EXCHANGE

Between Wytheville, Virginia,
and the North Carolina line,
he meets a wagon headed
where he's been, seated beside
her parents a dark-eyed girl
who grips the reins in her fist,
no more than sixteen, he'd guess
as they come closer and she
doesn't look away or blush
but allows his eyes to hold
hers that moment their lives pass.
He rides into Boone at dusk,
stops at an inn where he buys
his supper, a sleepless night
thinking of fallow fields still
miles away, the girl he might
not find the like of again.
When dawn breaks he mounts his roan,
then backtracks, searches three days
hamlets and farms, any smoke
rising above the tree line
before he heads south, toward home,
the French Broad's valley where spring
unclinches the dogwood buds
as he plants the bottomland,
come night by candlelight builds
a butter churn and cradle,

cherry headboard for the bed,
forges a double-eagle
into a wedding ring and then
back to Virginia and spends
five weeks riding and asking
from Elk Creek to Damascas
before he finds the wagon
tethered to the hitching post
of a crossroads stone, inside
the girl who smiles as if she'd
known all along his gray eyes
would search until they found her.
She asks one question, his name,
as her eyes study the gold
smoldering there between them,
the offered palm she lightens,
slips the ring on herself so
he knows right then the woman
she will be, bold enough match
for a man rash as his name.

A PREACHER WHO TAKES UP SERPENTS LAMENTS THE PRESENCE OF SKEPTICS IN HIS CHURCH

Every sabbath they come,
gawk like I'm something
in a tent at a county fair.
In the vanity of their unbelief
they will cover an eye with a camera
and believe it will make them see.
They see nothing. I show them Mark 16
but they believe in the word of man.
They believe death is an end.

And would live like maggots,
wallow in the filth of man's creation.
Less than a mile from here
the stench of sulphur rises
like fog off the Pigeon River.
They do not believe it a sign
of their own wickedness.
They cannot see a river
is a vein in God's arm.

When I open the wire cages
they back away like crayfish
and tell each other I am insane—
terrified I may not be.

Others, my own people, whisper
He tempts God, and will not join me.
They cannot understand surrender
is humility, not arrogance,
that a man afraid to die cannot live.

Only the serpents sense the truth.
The diamondback's blunted tale is silent,
the moccasin's pearl-white mouth closed.
The coral snake coils around
my wrist, a harmless bright bracelet,
in the presence of the Lord.

THE AFFLICTED

My elders would speak of those who could not,
whose vocabulary of verb and noun
never took root, grew sentences,
as afflicted, yet also blessed in
one way always significant.
Skill with saw, guitar or horse,
a strong back, pleasing face or just
a kind disposition would be enough.
Families back then would wait for years
for that one talent to come to light,
confirming the attentive eye,
the marked child marked with God's favor.

THE PREACHER IS CALLED
TO TESTIFY FOR THE ACCUSED

Before a just Lord raised this world's foundations,
centered the sun, speckled the heavens with stars,
before He dredged the land out of the water,
molded Adam's limbs from dust and spit,
God knew the time would come when Isaac Hampton
would drink too much one night but not before
he won in a poker game no gold or silver,
no ring or saddle but an owlshead pistol
he didn't want or need. Collateral
was all it was, all it *seemed* to be.
Then later when he dealt himself three kings,
and won a jug of whiskey it was clear
that deck was stacked though not by Isaac Hampton.
So instead of heading home as he intended,
and would have had the hoarfrost limned the ground,
he went instead to drink with Ezra Whitfield
down on the French Broad River's sandy banks
because no cold wind sent them home, no rain
fell from heaven until the morning came.
These are facts. They cannot be disputed.
We've all heard the sheriff's testimony.
The night was *strangely warm*, his words, not mine.
And why was Ezra on that riverbank,
a man not much for drink except this night?
His Brahma bull had died that afternoon.
As surely as He led us to this courtroom,
God had led that bull up to the springhouse

to gorge itself on laurel that would kill it
not three days before or three days after
November nineteenth, 1923.
That's why Ezra walked out of that hollow
on Sunday night when any other Sunday
he'd be in church, not off to town to try
and drink away the pain, the memory
of two months' sweat left in his neighbor's field
to buy a bull he'd only owned a week.
And though there were two paths he could have taken
he took the one that followed Middlefork
although the other path was better worn,
had fewer roots to trip on in the dark.
God brought Ezra Whitfield down that trail,
brought Isaac up from town, the moonshine whiskey
waiting to be drunk, the owlshead pistol
crouching like a panther in his pocket.
Isaac almost home, in five more minutes
he'd have left the river trail and followed
the creek up Dismal Mountain, which did not happen.
For they had crossed God's path. We know the rest,
or think we know, the drunken argument
the grievous wound. Ezra in the river.
We know no more than water spiders know
the depths of pools they skate across. Like them
we live upon the surface. Things occur
we have no inkling of. All we can know
is God's watch measured Ezra Whitfield's time

so Isaac Hampton's crime was our Lord's will,
which is no crime unless our pride would judge
the apple's fall, the barn owl's dark, clawed sight,
the weasel's fierce appetite, this son
I fathered so our Father's will might raise
a rusty owlshead pistol to the chest
of Ezra Whitfield, Isaac's closest friend.
Take it back a hundred generations,
all the way to He who begot Adam.
For there is where it ends, where it begins.
We must believe in providence and see
good where only evil seems to be.
If Judas had not kissed our savior's cheek
Christ would not have died on Calvary,
redeemed us with his blood. No earthly man
did a greater good. It's my belief
that Judas walks the golden paths of heaven.
These words I speak, they too are preordained
to sway or not to sway. If my son hangs
he dies like Judas died but unlike Judas
not by his own hand, condemned like Christ
by men who thought their actions justified.

SIGNS

My older kin always believed
in looking backward to explain
the here and now, always a sign
present in the past each time

a barn burned down, a life was lost.
So like boys turning over stones
to find what darkness hid from day,
they'd turn over in their minds

the way a mare shied from its stall
as if she smelled hay smoldering,
a living hand so damp and cold
it seemed already in the grave.

And so I learned to see the world
as language one might understand
but only when translated by
signs first forgotten or misread.

ANIMAL HIDES

As if in flight they ascend
on barn-back, shed-side: bobcat
and fox, raccoon and black bear,
limbs splayed as if gliding on
wind-lift as coats dry and tan
to become somehow more than
brags of well-hid trap, true aim,
a poor man's taxidermy—
for they remain when weathered
into fur-scrap, pelt-shadow
ghosting across graying boards,
as though their death-hurriers
kenned animals too had souls,
some essence that yet lingered,
must be earth-freed, given wing.

THE ASCENT

Some thought she had slipped, the plank
glazed slick with ice, or maybe
already cold beyond care,
drowsy and weary, bare feet
tempting a creekbed's promise
of sleep, though she struggled out,
her trail a handprint of stars
rising toward a dazzle of white
where sun and snow met. They found
her homespun dress, underclothes,
before they found her, her eyes
open as the sky, as cold,
as far away. Her father
climbed the nearest tree, brought down
green sprigs, berries bright as blood,
wove a garland for her brow,
and that was how they left her,
wearing a crown, unburied,
knowing they'd never hunt here
or build a homestead where she
undressed, left their world as death
closed around her like a room
and she lay down on the snow,
a bride awaiting her groom.

FROM *THE MABINOGION*

Having twice traveled the sea,
battle-bloodied, swords bone-dulled,
Branwen buried inside her
square-sided grave, having heard
the three birds of Rhiannon,
they came into a great hall—
sea-facing, hero worthy,
two doors wide open, one closed,
and like snow warmed by the sun
all they had seen and suffered
melted away. No sorrow
could harbor inside that hall.
No beard grayed, night and day merged
into vast fields of twilight
beyond time, though a time came
they chose to open the door.
The cold sea stung their faces.
Memory settled like ravens
upon their shoulders: kinsmen
and friends who died by their side,
woes of age, old wounds, heart grief
whose sudden weight so staggered
they wondered it ever borne,
and knew they were finally home.

IN A SPRINGHOUSE AT NIGHT

Candle-dim flickering shadows, orange
salamanders flare across floorstone,
water troughed, held like gutterswell.
Cabbage and beets, beans and sweet corn
fill the walls. Grandmother's tall
hands lighten shelves. My fingers braille
springflow verbing: unearthed, sprung.

BLUE RIVER

One Saturday afternoon
my father raised a paint brush,
to make the River Jordan
run through the Carolina hills.
I lay on a pew, followed
the whispered hymns the brush made
as it swept across the wall,
and that blue river rose high
as purple windows darkened
into bruises, root-shadows
seeped from the corners, deepened
the baptistry. It was like
my father drowned as his arm
reached up, finished the far shore,
as if his hand a last wave
before he sank in the pool
where grown men fell and gasped
while hallelujahs shook the church,
the place where I would fall too
on some soon-coming Sunday,
washed away in a current
raised by my father's right hand.

SPRING LIZARDS

We could not keep them in jars
with star-pricked lids or fishhook
their lips, cast them into the
deep pools of Middlefork Creek,
though we might gently hold
the rough-skinned newts, mud puppies,
sleek salamanders, ours for
a few seconds, then set free,
sipped under rusty tin that
roofed the spring's source, the hidden
earth-water we'd always heard
their presence had blessed, made pure.

WATERSHED

I could not see, even say
what it was my aunt explained
with a word, a nod beyond
the slant of pasture, the end
of family land. I supposed
a weave of wood and tin used
by thirsty hunters, maybe
the lost, or a child like me
willing to straddle barbed wire,
go where just sky rose higher,
to find nothing built, instead
a barn-tall rock whose face shed
slow streams of water like tears
I let fall on my fingers,
like the blind girl whose first word
flowed out from the underworld
through well-pump onto her hand
before it could be sounded.

GINSENG

Even midday the mountain's
north face was veiled in shadows,
a place to stay lost, as once
an old woman had, her ghost
still trying to get back home,
where others lived. It was here
my grandfather searched each fall
the deep coves, the gloam under
cliffhangs where yellow leaves pooled
so bright it seemed what sun had
scattered in since spring was held
until October, then freed
to light the virid stem-wings
into a brief golden star.
I went with him once, our words
kept low, almost a whisper
as we shook free the pale roots
from black loam, planted the seeds
and headed home, stone stepping
where two boulders squeezed the creek
to a slick white rush, crossed there
where no ghost dared to follow.

LASTING WATER

After fingers raked out the caul
of black leaves, and spring lizards
skittered once exposed like things
lifted by the wind, only then
would my grandfather savor
that spurt water makes in sand
as it breaks free from the world's
underneath to pool and spread
across the land like skyroots
even in the direst drought.
He called it *lasting water,*
that low-pulsed flow he scooped up
with blistered palms so it might
touch his lips as he kneeled there
at the field's edge where corn rows
withered like paper in flames,
limp rags of tobacco burned
without a match and green wings
sang in the trees to bring rain.

PASSAGE

Even raised from their lost world,
captured in *Life*'s late-fifties
suburban gloss, those cave prints
kept their power—animals
flowing like strange dreams across
veldts of limestone, human hand
hovering on the wall like flame,
something untranslatable
no camera could bring to light,
so that spring I searched the cave
above Goshen Creek, my lamp
wood-wick burning to thumb
before dropped, another struck,
waved over walls like a brush,
but no sabertooth, bison
muscled that dark, nothing there
but a hunter's old campfire,
so I let my last match die,
imagined walls come alive,
hoof and paw circling, one hand
raised among them in welcome.

BARN LOFT: 1959

So still I can hear the heat
sear the tin, the barn swallow
weave its nest out of slant-light.
From shadows that smell like straw,
I watch corn rows ripple far
as Parkson's Cove, the scarecrow
raises his arms, wades the green waves,
and that word the preacher spoke
comes clear through the July haze
as though the writing spider
has caught time, suspended there
between an E and a Y.

THE FOX

Two months before he died my uncle saw
a red fox near the field edge where he plowed,
watching him, its tongue unpanting though
the August heat-haze waved the air like water.

That night he claimed it was his father, then laughed
as if he wasn't serious, as if
all summer long we hadn't watched his face
grow old too quick, gray-stubbled, sudden-lined.

His wife would try the last days that he lived
to get him to the hospital but he
took to his bed, awaited the approach
of padded feet, coming close, then closer.

AUGUST 1959:
MORNING SERVICE

Beside the open window
on the cemetery side,
I drowsed as Preacher Lusk gripped
his Bible like a bat snagged
from the pentecostal gloom.
In that room where heat clabbered
like churned butter, my eyes closed,
freed my mind into the light
on the window's other side,
followed the dreamy bell-ring
of Randy Ford's cows across
Licklog Creek to a spring pool
where orange salamanders swirled
and scuttled like flames. It was
not muttered words that brought me
back to that church, nor was it
the hard comfort of pews rowed
like the gravestones of my kin,
but the a cappella hymn
sung by my great-aunt, this years
before the Smithsonian
taped her voice as if the song
of some vanishing species,
which it was, which all songs are,
years before the stroke wrenched her
face into a gnarled silence,

this morning before all that
she led us across Jordan,
and the gravestones leaned as if
even the dead were listening.

ABANDONED HOMESTEAD
IN WATAUGA COUNTY

All that once was is this,
shattered glass, a rot
of tin and wood, the hum
of limp-legged wasps that ascend
like mote swirls in the heatlight.

Out front a cherry tree
buckles in fruit, harvested
by yellow jackets and starlings,
the wind, the rain, and the sun.

AMONG THE BELIEVERS

Even the young back then died old.
My great-aunt's brow at twenty-eight
was labored by a hardscrabble world
no final breath could smooth away.
They laid her out in her wedding dress,
the life that killed in her arms, the head
turned to suckle her cold breast
in eternity. A cousin held
a camera over an open casket,
cast a shadow the camera raised
where flesh and wood and darkness met,
a photograph the husband claimed.
Nailed on the wall above his bed,
smudged and traced for five decades,
a cross of shadow, shadowing death,
across an uncomprehending face.

GOOD FRIDAY 1995,
DRIVING WESTWARD

This day I feel I live among strangers.
The old blood ties beckon so I drive west
to Buncombe County, a weedy graveyard
where my rare last name crumbles on stone.

All were hardshell Baptists, farmers
who believed the soul is another seed
that endures when flesh and blood are shed,
that all things planted rise toward the sun.

I dream them shaking dirt off strange new forms.
Gathered for the last harvest, they hold hands,
take their first dazed steps toward heaven.

EUREKA MILL

INVOCATION

This late night I spread
a fraying Springmaid bedsheet
across the kitchen table.
In the almost silence
of house-creak and time's
persistent tracking of eternity,
I unscrew the mason jar,
pool the lid with moonshine,
flare the battered cigarette lighter.
A blue trembling rises from liquid
expanding finally to smoke,
all elements merging tonight,
whispering out the window,
curling northward to seep six feet
into the black bony dirt
and guide his spirit across
the declining mountains here,
where I sit and sip, await
a tobacco-breathed haint, shadowless shadow,
bloodless blood-kin I have summoned
to hear my measured human prayer:
Grandfather guide my hand
to weave with words a thread
of truth as I write down
your life and other lives,
close kin but strangers too,

those lives all lived as gears
in Springs' cotton mill
and let me not forget
your lives were more than that.

EUREKA

Here was no place   for illumination
the cotton dust thick   window-strained light.
The metal squall drowned   what could not be shouted
everything geared   warping and filling.

Though surely there were   some times that he paused
my grandfather thinking   *This is my life*
and catching himself   before he was caught
lost wages or fingers   the risk of reflection.

Or another recalled   in those reckoning moments
remembering the mountains   the hardscrabble farm
where a workday as long   bought no guarantee
of money come fall   full bellies in winter.

To earn extra pay   each spring he would climb
the mill's water tower   repaint every letter.
That vowel heavy word   defined the horizon
a word my grandfather   could not even read.

IN A DRY TIME

My crops were dying in the field.
The dog days seemed to never end.
I'd wait and curse and pray but still
nothing but the well bucket fell.
Soon it would scrape bottom. By then
my crops would stand dead in the field.
September came in dry as hell.
The sun never blinked, no hint of a wind.
I'd pray and curse and pray but still
not even Jesus Christ could heal
dirt turned to dust, scorched roots. By then
my crops were standing dead in the field.
I had no harvest to pay my bills,
so tried for another loan and when
the bank said sorry I begged but still
it did no good, though my eyes filled
with water, too little water to mend
broken crops dead in the field.
I left crop rows for rows of steel.

MILL VILLAGE

Mill houses lined both sides of every road
like boxcars on a track. They were so close
a man could piss off his own front porch,
hit four houses if he had the wind.

Every time your neighbors had a fight,
then made up in bed as couples do,
came home drunk, played the radio,
you'd know, whether or not you wanted to.

So I bought a dimestore picture, a country scene,
built a frame and nailed it on the wall,
no people in it, just a lot of land,
stretching out behind an empty barn.

Sometimes at night if I was feeling low,
I'd stuff my ears with cotton. Then I'd stare
up at that picture like it was a window,
and I was back home listening to the farm.

But what was done was done. Before too long
the weave room jarred the hearing from my ears,
and I got used to living with a crowd.
Before too long I took the picture down.

LOW WATER

In August when the dog days came we'd check
the water in the morning and after our shift,
eyes searching for the first sign of the rock
that sprouted in midriver that time of year.

We called that rock the Colonel's Colonel. It was
the one thing in the county that bossed him.
If that rock showed three days we had it made
and knew it soon would be low water time.

That's when the water in the millrace fell.
The machines got tired as us and finally stalled.
There was nothing else that Colonel Springs could do
but let us go, at least a little while.

Out in the yard someone would play guitar.
We'd sing "Rock of Ages" or some other hymn,
or sleep until the water gained up again,
and the whistle blew and we'd have to go back in.

It was an easy time. That hour or two
made mill work tolerable. At night we'd pray
for another week of blue sky afternoons,
at least until the drought of twenty-one.

When no rain came for a month, we thought of kin
back in the mountains praying hard as us
for crops that withered as dirt turned to dust.
Each of us praying for the other's misery.

That's when we knew the world was truly evil,
and after work we'd watch the cottonmouths
sunning on the rock we thought a savior,
taking their ease, fat come rain or drought.

SPRING FEVER

Each spring you knew when it was planting time.
The men would get more careless on the job
and have that faraway look in their eyes.
You'd know they were behind a mule and plow.

They'd drink a lot more whiskey that time of year,
and take a lot less from their section boss,
who like us wives knew it the better course
to cut them slack until the fever passed.

But they were just remembering the best,
not the things they'd gladly left behind,
that made them leave. It's easy to love a life
you only have to live the good parts of.

They'd forgotten what a late-spring hailstorm does
in fifteen minutes' time to six weeks' work,
how long it took a hay-filled barn to burn,
when a lantern spilled its flame or lightning struck.

They'd forgotten the loneliness, the days
you wouldn't speak a word from dawn to dusk
except to cows and chickens and felt your tongue
was rusting like a plowshare in the rain.

But maybe deep inside they did remember.
They must have because every March you'd hear
men swear come planting time next spring they'd be
back in the fields. They'd say that every year.

ACCIDENT

We were running speed frames. Mary knew
those flyers could snatch an apron off or break
a bone like a twig given half a chance.
But her baby had been sick, kept her awake
three nights in a row. She was so tired
she barely kept her head up. When she didn't
those flyers grabbed her hair, would not let go
until her scalp came too. I guess she screamed
though who could hear her over the machines.
I never knew a body held so much blood,
or ever wanted to know. Worse than it looks
the shift boss said, and helped her to his car.
Mary was back at work that afternoon.
She didn't want to lose a half day's wage.
After the bandages came off she wore
a wig she ordered from a catalog,
and never slept on the job again.

THE SWEEPER

Ma died when I was very young.
After that it wasn't long
I went into the mill to sweep,
came home for supper and for sleep.

Dad shaved my head the lint was so bad,
but I didn't cry because he said
I was the oldest child and so
must grow up faster than he'd hoped.

On winter mornings when I walked
in darkness to the mill I thought
of what Dad said and I was proud
of being a man, of helping out.

And helping other people too,
folks we made those sheets for who
still slept in what I helped to make,
still slept as I walked into work.

THE FAMOUS PHOTOGRAPHER
VISITS EUREKA

That yankee photographer would stop
each time a smile or laugh slipped out.
Be serious, he said. *This means*
much more than you can understand.
I'd climb back on the stool to reach
the frame, to work more "seriously,"
while he hid behind the camera,
reduced my life to grays and blacks.

Decades later I realized why
he'd cropped the child out of that scene,
read how his photographs had changed
the labor laws across the South,
and knew no one should ever care
he denied me my humanity.

BEARINGS

He's scraped manure off his boots a last time,
filled the front room with what he has chosen
to keep on owning. He's alone, his uncle gone,
gearing back through the hills upwinding into
the gasping curves and drops of the mountains.

He stands on the porch, no work until tomorrow,
millhouses planted like corn rows each way he
looks, Eureka's water tower rising above as if
a hard high-legged scarecrow. He steps down on
the strange level road, walks west toward town.

He finds a grill, asks for what he's memorized:
a hamburger and a Coke and his change. Outside
in the loud afternoon, he stares into windows
until he sees shoes. The clerk takes his bills
and grins when my grandfather asks for a poke.

He walks out toward Eureka's smoke and rumble,
toward the millhouses crouched and huddled in
the mill's shadow, and soon finds he is lost.
Each house might be his or maybe the next one,
and he walks an hour before he finally asks.

He tells the man he is looking for James Rash,
a friend who's just moved here. The man says
Tommy Singleton got fired last week. I'd bet
that's where your friend is at and points to
a house, and so my grandfather found himself.

He stayed inside till the whistle woke him up,
and threw his boots on the roof so they might
guide him back those first evenings and later
the Saturday nights he weaved under moonshine,
searching roof after roof trying to find home.

JOKES

The best was that if Hoover ever died
and six pallbearers took him to his grave,
he'd rise up in his coffin and he'd swear
four men could do the job as easily.

That joke was told in thirty-one. By then
the owners had us stretched like rubber bands,
and they would fire us if we dared complain,
and Hoover told the owners that was fine.

To have some meat on Sundays we would shoot
some gray squirrels in the woods below the mill.
We'd call them Hoover hogs, another joke
we filled our mouths with so we could go on.

THE STRETCH-OUT

I was only seventeen, a girl
who still could trust a suit and smile.
Let's see how fast these looms will run,
he said, a stopwatch in his palm.

Those first nights when I got back home
I swear I could barely raise my fork.
I'd fall asleep with my work clothes on,
still weary when the whistle blew.

The child inside me felt it too,
and right then seemed to just give up.
I felt its life bleed out of me.
I cried but I cried quietly

and let the bed sheets clot and stain,
so that my man and me might save
what strength a full night's sleep might give.
I closed my eyes and slept again.

FLYING SQUADRON

It was a dangerous time. From dawn to dusk
we rode from mill to mill to spread the word.
We were cursed and shouted at. Sometimes
things got more serious. We carried scars
from fists and clubs, left some friends behind
in Gaston County, down in Honea Path,
shot by the owners' thugs or bayoneted
by frightened kids in National Guard uniforms.
At night we'd build a campfire by the road.
We'd talk and laugh and sing our union songs.
Later with a young man at our side,
we might get up and leave the campfire's glow,
find a pine straw bed to lie down on,
and prove two bodies rubbed together can
spark up heat as well. It felt so good
to breathe fresh air instead of cotton dust,
to be outside that spinning room awhile.
We knew we'd never be so brave again.

THE BALLAD OF ELLA MAE WIGGINS

It was the fourteenth of September
in nineteen hundred and twenty-nine,
when she made her last stand in a cottonfield
a few miles from the South Carolina line.
We won't forget the day
strikebreakers struck poor Ella Mae down.

They shot her in the chest and let her die,
then took her body into town.
She was just a linthead on this earth
but in heaven she'll wear a crown.
We won't forget the day
strikebreakers struck poor Ella Mae down.

Oh mothers tell your children this sad tale
so they will tell their children when they're grown.
She sacrificed her life to save the union.
Eureka workers, she was one of your own.
So don't forget the day
strikebreakers struck poor Ella Mae down.

1934

After the union men left town,
Old Man Springs stood by the gate.
He tried to gauge us by our eyes,
unsure whose side we now were on.

As if we knew. It sounded good
what organizers promised us,
a shorter day, a better wage,
a worker getting to boss the boss.

They told us that it was our sweat
that bought the mansion Springs lived in.
The time had come to share the wealth,
they said, *we've got them on the run.*

But when the other mills laid off,
Springs made sure we had some work.
We'd watch warehouses fill with cloth
we knew there was no market for.

What did we owe him for those jobs?
A tough question, though not as tough
as how on earth we'd feed our kids
if strikers shut Eureka down.

When a flying squadron headed south
and crossed the Chester County line,
we left our shift to walk outside.
We filled our fists to welcome them.

BLACK AND WHITE

One December Colonel Springs dressed down
in overalls himself, his children and wife,
the idea being to create a Christmas card
sure to make his business partners laugh.
The chauffeur drove them to the mill, the photographer
already inside, setting up his camera.

The Colonel placed himself behind a cart
filled up with bobbins, arms taut, brow creased.
His wife stood behind him, her hair tied back
to authenticate the blank look on her face.
The children too pretended they were working,
leaned their lean bodies against a machine.

The photograph turned out a shade too dark
to satisfy the photographer who blamed
a lack of proper lighting, the jolt and jar
of machinery that hurt his concentration.
But Colonel Springs was pleased and always swore
that Lewis Hine could not have done it better.

BOUNDARIES

She thought that her beauty   brought her a way out.
She thought she could live   like she wasn't a linthead
spend time with a man   whose hands were uncalloused.

Her coat and best dress   were kept in her locker.
She'd head straight to town   when our shift had ended.
When she saw us there   she pretended she didn't.

She would not deny us.   We took care of that
bringing men with us   to handle her beau.
We waited in shadows   until they walked by.

My sisters held her   while my hawkbill knife
stripped off her fine dress   cropped her fine hair.
Her town boy felt fists   lost most of his smile.

She understood then.   Her sweetheart did too.
Her belly still swelled.   There was no stopping that
or stopping the words that weren't even whispered.

Some men, unmarried,   helped her make production
though none of them offered   to give her their name.

REVENANT

Below our backyards that crumbled
each day a little more
their puny allotments into
a Springmaid riverbed where
no river ran, the crossties
laid out like coffins to bridge
a flow of forged steel,
there on those train tracks
our lives flashed before us,
rolls of Eureka gray cloth
shrouded in boxcars, leaving
Chester for Lancaster's
Grace finishing plant.
Twice a night we waked
when our millhouses rattled,
finally resettling as if
the die had been cast.

BROWN LUNG

Sometimes I'd spend the whole night coughing up
what I'd been breathing in all day at work.
I'd sleep in a chair or take a good stiff drink,
anything to get a few hours' rest.

The doctor called it asthma and suggested
I find a different line of work as if
a man who had no land or education
could find himself another way to live.

For that advice I paid a half-day's wage.
Who said advice is cheap? It got so bad
each time I got a break at work I'd find
the closest window, try to catch a breath.

My foreman was a decent man who knew
I'd not last much longer on that job.
He got me out of that dusty room,
let me load boxcars in the yard.

But even though I slept more I'd still wake
gasping for air at least one time a night,
and when I dreamed I dreamed of bumper crops
of Carolina cotton in my chest.

PLANE CRASH

When we heard the Colonel's son was dead
at twenty-one, burned up so bad
they had to check his dental charts
with what was left to get a match,
we first believed it wasn't true.
Such things as that were not supposed
to happen to any folks but us.
The next day he was back at work
and never showed his son had died,
so we said nothing, let him pass,
glad he understood the need
for him to act like even death
could never make him one of us.

LISTENING TO WBT

All you had to do was turn the knob
until the light clicked on and soon you'd find
rising out of static was your life.
Every time you heard "The Weave Room Blues"
or "Cotton Mill Colic No. 3" you felt
like a deer that risked a meadow, its eyes
lifted to see the barrel too late.
Someone had caught you in his sights,
hit you solid in the guts
with all the things that you had thought
you didn't want to think too long about.
But days later you'd catch yourself
humming those lines as you worked your shift.
Maybe it was the banjo and guitar,
the way they prettied up the words,
that made those songs lift up your heart
same as a Sunday morning hymn.
Or maybe in the end it was the words,
the bare-assed truth making a stand
in a voice that could have been your own.

LAST INTERVIEW

That's an early portrait on the wall,
painted the year I graduated from
Princeton University, the year
I took my first trip to the continent,
a disappointment, except for the wines.
But I digress. You spoke of exploitation,
the working man's abuse by men like me.
If they are so abused why don't they go
back to the farms they flee to work in mills,
become Vanderbilt Agrarians
quoting Cicero as they slop their hogs.
In thirty-four when the union leaders came
and promised everything they could, then more,
my workers stuck with me. My workers knew
I'd take care of them. Eureka ran
when other mills shut down. I took a loss
so they could have some work. Noblesse oblige
an idea we still live by in the South.
All Men created equal? Yes, perhaps
but see how soon we sort the top ones out.
Watch any group of children, they have leaders,
followers and stragglers. It does not change
as they grow older. No one questions rank
in war or politics so why not business,
though you'll argue otherwise. I've watched your pen.
It hasn't moved since this interview began.
You'll slant what I have said to fit your needs.

I know how writers work, their luxury
of always being outside looking in,
passing easy judgments while they risk
nothing of their own, mere dilettantes.
Your words mean nothing to me. I know the truth.
I gave them more than they ever had before.

FIRST SHIFT

The four thirty whistle won't wake him this morning.
My father's awake, dreaming of paychecks.
Bedsprings creak in the other bedroom,
my grandfather coughing, my grandmother rising.
Then the clatter of pans, the warm smell of coffee,
the dog at the door, begging for scraps.

The three of them walk up the hill in the dark,
across the train tracks, past Darby's Grill.
They pass through the gate where I cannot follow,
except in blood-memory, except in the knowledge
I eat well and I rest on the gift of their labors.

PHOTOGRAPH OF MY PARENTS OUTSIDE EUREKA COTTON MILL. DATED JUNE 1950

Back against the chain-link fence,
my father's muscled left arm twists
like vine that sprouts a wire-meshed fist.
My mother leans into his chest.
She's known him a month, cannot guess
what I will see, at least not yet,
in my father's odd pose, the fingerless
awkward clutch of metal, as if
caught in Eureka's sprung-steel grip.

JULY 1949

This is what I cannot remember—
a young woman stooped in a field,
the hoe callousing her hands,
the rows stretching out like hours.
And this woman, my mother, rising
to dust rising half a mile
up the road, the car
she has waited days for
realized in the trembling heat.

It will rust until spring, the hoe
dropped at the field's edge.
She is running toward the car,
the sandlapper relatives who spill out
coughing mountain air with lint-filled lungs,
running toward the half-filled grip
she will learn to call a suitcase.

She is dreaming another life,
young enough to believe
it can only be better—
indoor plumbing, eight-hour shifts, a man
who waits unknowing for her, a man
who cannot hear through the weave room's
roar the world's soft click,
fate's tumblers falling into place,
soft as the sound of my mother's
bare feet as she runs,
runs toward him, toward me.

WAKING

FIRST MEMORY

Dragonflies dip, rise. Their backs
catch light, purple like church glass.
Gray barn planks balance on stilts,
walk toward the pond's deep end.
A green smell simmers shallows,
where tadpoles flow like black tears.
Minnows lengthen their shadows.
Something unseen stirs the reeds.

THE TROUT IN THE SPRINGHOUSE

Caught by my uncle
in the Watauga River,
brought back in a bucket
because some believed
its gills were like filters,
that pureness poured into
the springhouse's trough pool,
and soon it was thriving
on sweet corn and biscuits,
guarding that spring-gush,
brushing my fingers
as I swirled the water
up in my palm cup
tasted its quickness
swimming inside me.

MILKING TRACES

The paths between pasture, barn
were no straight lines but slow curves
around a hill that centered
thirty acres. To a child
those narrow levels seemed like
belts worn on the hill's bulged waist,
if climbed straight up, tall steps for
stone Aztec ruins—though razed
each time dawnlight peaked landrise,
belts and steps became sudden
contrails from planets circling
the sun's blaze, planets disguised
with cow hide, the furrowed skin
of an old woman's visage.

SLEEPWALKING

Strange how I never once woke
in a hall, on a porch step,
but always outside, bare feet
slick with dew-grass, the house
deeper shadow, while above
the moon leaned its round shoulder
on a white oak's limbs, stars spread
skyward like fistfuls of jacks.
Rising as if from water
was the way dark lightened,
slow-returning, reluctant,
as though while I'd been sleeping
summoned away to attend
matters other than a child's
need for a world to be in.

JUNK CAR IN SNOW

No shade tree surgery could
revive its engine, so rolled
into the pasture, left stalled
among cattle, soon rust-scabs
breaking out on blue paint, tires
sagging like leaky balloons,
yet when snow came, magical,
an Appalachian igloo
I huddled inside, cracked glass
my window as the snow smoothed
the pasture as though a quilt
for winter to rest upon,
and how quiet it was—the creek
muffled by ice, gray squirrels
curled in leaf beds, the crows mute
among stark lifts of branches,
only the sound of my own
white breath dimming the window.

TIME FLOW

Green plush of bank moss, a smell
like after rain, and the creek
deepening behind the shed
where Nolan White spent his time
to wedge hours and seconds
out of time, free them to spill
out the open door as if
another current flowing
through the pool where I sank worms
to raise watery rainbows.
His one son had died, so now
he worked alone, making clocks
for Boone tourists. Once I laid
down my tackle, stepped inside
a moth-swirl of ticks and chimes,
at the center latched chestnut
laid upon two sawhorses,
what Nolan White bent over,
hands dipping in, attentive
as a surgeon as he set
each gear in place. When it stirred
he brought me close, let me hear
that one pulse among many.

WATAUGA COUNTY: 1959

On Clay Ridge a crescent moon
balanced itself, soon became
an open parenthesis
no father, uncle could close
as we hunched on farmhouse steps,
wore Sunday clothes days early,
what conversation the rasp
of matches. Small blades of flame
rose to faces no tears marked
as I heard silence widen
like fish swirls on a calm pond,
touch the last fence he had strung,
the tractor in the far field
already starting to rust.

BONDING FIRE

For Bob Cumming

A spark takes hold in a glen
in Scotland's midlands and burns
winter and summer, and when
hands rending that spark grow cold

passed on to daughter and son
fire passed hearth to hearth to fire
a bride's wedding night passion,
light an old man's corpse candle,

part heirloom, part talisman,
cradled and nursed like a child
in the ship's hold when the clan
sailed west to Charleston, then west

to east Tennessee, the fire
carried by wagon, by hand,
huddled by when a panther
cried out at night or when night

turned slantland white when they came
into the Blue Ridge where they
raised their hearths over a flame
two centuries old, two more

passing until water came
to douse that valley, to douse
the hearth of one who remained
to tend that fire, who refused

to leave the valley until
that fire left with him, the truck's
windows left up lest wind still
the pail of sparks his lap held.

POCKETKNIVES

Carried like time, consulted
as often when the sermon
droned on past noon, hay bailer
broke a chain, any other
lingering moments their scarred
and calloused workflesh idled,
the blades pried free the way wives
might slip a ribbon, that same
delicate tug when forge-craft
sharpened what light sun or bulb
provided as they trimmed dirt
from the undersides of nails,
surfaced splinters, bled blisters,
a tool but more than a tool
each time they rasped a whetstone
across steel until it flashed
pure as silver, then a rag
doused in oil to rub new-bright
the handles hewed from antler,
pearl, hardwood and ivory
laced with brass or gold, the one
vanity of men caught once
when dead in a coat and tie,
so ordered from catalogs,
saved and traded for, searched for
in sheds and fields if lost, passed
father to son as heirlooms,
like talismans carried close

though most times, cloaked as the hearts
of these men who rarely spoke
their fears and hopes, let their words
clench inside a locked silence.

SHADETREE

After Sunday noon-dinner
men gathered where truck or car
motor hung from an oak limb
like some trophy shot or yanked
from woods or river, and though
all had their views on just how
and what needed to be done,
not one man rolled up his sleeves.
Cigarette butts and brown spit
marked an afternoon's passing
as each held his place as if
before a hearth, the log-chained
weld of steel hanging sometimes
for a month, huddled around
so it might spark and fuel
an allowance of language
beyond utility, though
always first the lexicon
of engines before slow shift
to story, joke and sometimes
the hotwired valves and pistons
making racket in the heart.

CAR TAGS

I have seen them as spare parts
on combines and hay balers,
poor man's wind chimes, a scarecrow's
loud jewelry, though my uncle
nailed his to the barn as if
patchwork armor, and after
five decades those rows of tin
lined up like a calendar
of one man's life weathering
sun and rain, mountain winters,
years rubbing away as rust
made the past harder to read
on heartwood warped and buckling
under the burden of time.

SPILLCORN

The road is now a shadow
of a road, overgrown with
blackjack oak, scrub pine. Years back
one of my kinsmen logged here,
a man needing steady work
no hailstorm or August drought
could take away, so followed
Spillcorn Creek into the gorge,
brought with him a mule and sled,
a Colt revolver to kill
the rattlesnakes, and always
tucked in his lunch sack a book:
history, sometimes a novel
from the Marshall library,
so come midday he might rest
his spine against bark and read
what had roughed his hands now smooth
as his fingertips turned
the leaves, each word whispered soft
as the wind reading the trees.

EMRYS

Lamp and candle, a lantern
fetched from the barn not enough,
more light needed to fling back
shadow-quilts on the birth-bed,
labor a breech child to life,
so the husband sent horseback
from Dismal Gorge, riding north
toward Blowing Rock, Joe Black's farm,
the one car close by, and soon
that Model T bumping down
logging roads thinned to cow paths,
light hauled deep into Dismal
like two long lengths of lumber—
and finally there, the cabin's
one door propped, light flooding in
as the doctor probes and cuts,
men turn their heads while women
heat water, bring out clean cloths,
and just before dawn a child
brought forth blinking and squalling,
the great-aunt speaking one word
carried deep in blood-memory,
crossing time and an ocean
to name this child born of light.

MIRROR

Ordered from Winston-Salem,
hauled by train far as Lenoir,
unboxed, bundled in blankets,
wagoned north to Blowing Rock,
jolted across Middlefork,
geed and hawed uphill while hands
braced it from sliding where land
slanted sharp as a barn roof,
before finally there, and then
brought through doors like a body,
unwrapped and uprighted so
after five years of breaking
land that had tried to break her,
after eight children, so long
seeing her face only in
wrinkles of water, she'll stand
free of her bedclothes, alone
inside the mirror's embrace,
let face, breasts, child-widened hips
come clear in first light and find
only herself, which is all
she wishes for this moment.

WOMAN AMONG LIGHTNING:
CATAWBA COUNTY FAIR, 1962

Tendrils of neon sprouting
sudden as kudzu across
seven acres of sawdust,
in the middle a great wheel
dredging buckets of darkness
out of the sky, and this night
wind flapping tents, cloud bellies
soon glowing like blown coals while
thundering their heavy freight
toward the fairground as riders
disembark early, but she
refuses, so rides into
the storm, her hands reaching up
as if to place on her head
the night's bright crown, this farmwife
leaving the ground where her days
are measured in rows, the hoe
swinging like a metronome
as life leaks away like blood
on land always wanting more,
wanting more, free of it now
as the hawk she saw at dawn,
wings embracing an updraft,
how it hovered that moment
above the fields and fence wire,
as she does now at the pause
between ascent and return,
far from earth as a fistful
of hard-earned quarters can take her.

BLOODROOT

Two weeks without frost will bloom
trout lily and bloodroot while
sun soaking through gorge-rocks stirs
the gorgon heads underneath,
unknotting, rising through veins
in granite, split tongues tasting
live air, divining heat-spill
where outcrops pool the noon sun
and I come with my snake stick,
work my way upridge. They pay
by the foot, those holy fools
who hold them on Sunday nights,
holy fools, I call them though
I was one too, before years
away at Bible College,
schooling they helped pay for so
I could better learn the Word,
learned instead the world, returned
a felled angel, my God now
a bottle of Jack Daniel's
held like prayer, my service
work I find when someone needs
barbed wire strung up, sheet rock hung,
whatever else gets the bills
in Randy Davidson's hand,
liquor rising behind him
like Jacob's Ladder, the ring
of his register sweeter

than a preacher's altar call.
Serpents pay best, satinbacks
old folks call them, big ones sell
for fifty bucks so each spring
I climb this ridge, always hear
the hum of resurrection
as I near, the pillowcase
filling with a muscled flow
like water in a suckhole,
and when I've caught all I can,
take them to Reverend Barlowe,
who does not know I listen
beneath the window those nights
he and the congregation kneel,
pray for my back-sliding soul,
then raise their serpents and I
raise mine that it might crawl down
my throat, settle and coil,
still the rattling in my heart.

THE REAPING

As supper cools, fireflies spark
dew-grass like stars on a pond
and still the hay baler hums
in the meadow, and he knows
what keeps his son in the field's
gathering darkness, so steps
through barbed wire strung in April,
already sagged by fence posts
leaned like cornstalks after hail
because the boy would not
listen, would always search for
shortcuts, even as a child
leaving weeds between bean rows,
cheating on nails when a shed
needed shingles, each shortcut
leading to this evening when
his father smells blood sizzling
on the metal and as he
frees an arm from the roller
chides his son for half a life
lost to save half a minute,
before kissing the cold brow,
forgiving what the reaper cannot.

ELEGY FOR MERLE WATSON

Nothing's on the level in this terrain.
A tractor loses its balance quick as a heart.
One tractor wheel turns in the morning light.
One hand clutches the earth, trying to hold on.
"Wayfaring Stranger," "Deep River Blues,"
those fatalistic mountain hymns became you.

Tonight your father cradles his guitar.
A stage half-empty confirms what we don't hear,
what does not echo, fill the runs and lines.
Musician, distant kin, your silence survives.

WHITE WINGS

Tucked in each pew's back pocket,
hymnals simmered in mote-light
until Sundays when the soiled
rough hands of farmers lifted
those songbibles, pages spread
like white wings being set free,
but what rose was one voice
woven from many, and heard
by Jason Storey who stood
in a field half an acre
of gravestones away, mute as
a fence post while neighbors sang
inside the church doors he swore
never to pass through after
wife and son died in childbirth,
that long-ago Christmas when
three days of snow made the road
to Blowing Rock disappear,
the doctor brought on horseback
arriving too late. Decades
Jason Storey would remain
true to his word, yet was there
in that field come rain or cold,
but came no closer, between
church and field two marble stones,
angel-winged, impassible.

RESONANCE

No rain for weeks, White Ash Creek
a dry scab, lake miles away,
nothing but flame, smoke, and heat,
kept at bay by men blackfaced

as miners after a shift,
including those who will see
myth-dreams awakened, a trout
alive in a burning tree,

branch-caught by the gill, closing
and opening its mouth as though
the smoke a murky upstream
it has to make its way through

to reach the hundred gallon
sky pool it spilled from, and when
flames flagshift, the trout is gone
back into *The Mabinogion*.

THREE A.M. AND
THE STARS WERE OUT

When the phone rings way too late
for good news, just another
farmer wanting me to lose
half a night's sleep and drive some
backcountry washout for miles,
fix what he's botched, on such nights
I'm like an old, drowsy god
tired of answering prayers,
so let it ring awhile, hope
they might hang up, though of course
they don't, don't because they know
the younger vets shuck off these
dark expeditions to me,
thinking it's my job, not theirs,
because I've done it so long
I'm used to such nights, because
old as I am I'll still do
what they refuse to, and soon
I'm driving out of Marshall
headed north, most often toward
Shelton Laurel, toward some barn
where a calf that's been bad-bred
to save stud fees is trying
to be born, or a cow laid
out in a barn stall, dying
of milk fever, easily cured
if a man hadn't wagered

against his own dismal luck,
waited too late, hoping to
save my fee for a salt lick,
roll of barbed wire, and it's not
all his own fault, poor too long
turns the smartest man stupid,
makes him see nothing beyond
a short-term gain, which is why
I know more likely than not
I'll be arriving too late,
what's to be done best done with
rifle or shotgun, so make
driving the good part, turn off
my radio, let the dark
close around until I know
a kind of loneliness that
doesn't feel sad as I pass
the homes of folks I don't know,
may never know, but wonder
what they are dreaming, what life
they wake to—thinking such things,
or sometimes just watching for
what stays unseen except on
country roads after midnight,
the copperheads soaking up
what heat the blacktop still holds,
foxes and bobcats, one time
in the fifties a panther,

yellow eyes bright as truck beams,
black-tipped tail swishing before
leaping away through the trees,
back into its extinction,
all this thinking and watching
keeping my mind off what waits
up on the road, worst of all
the calves I have to pull one
piece at a time, birthing death.
Though sometimes it all works out.
I turn a calf's head and then
like a safe's combination
the womb unlocks, calf slides free,
or this night when stubborn life
got back on its feet, round eyes
clear and hungry, my I.V.
stuck in its neck, and I take
my time packing up, ask for
a second cup of coffee,
so I can linger awhile
in the barn mouth watching stars
awake in their wide pasture.

GENEALOGY

From Wales to Murderkill Hundred, then
in one generation down the Shenandoah,
to North Carolina where tombstones raised
a topography of accident and will
across three mountain counties, otherwise
crossing only centuries. Perhaps
some racial memory held them there—
an isolate people, a name carried far
only in the wind's harsh sibilance,
its branch-lashing rattle and rush.

THE CODE

The code said any man who asked received
more than food and shelter, safety too,
so when a stranger came out of the night
with bloodstains on his shirt, MacGregor knew
what his obligations were and shared
his hearth and meat and whiskey. Soon enough
a pack of hounds leaped baying at the door,
with them men who wore MacGregor tartan,
kin seeking one who killed one of their own.
The old man turned them back into the dark,
then led his guest across the hills to where
a boat could be procured. Upon that shore
one favor would be asked, a favor granted.
MacGregor dipped the shirt into the loch,
rinsed his only son's blood from the cloth.

THE CROSSING

Fog never lifts, though the days
pass as he makes his way home
from Shiloh, the peach orchard
where, left for dead, he awoke

shrouded in petals, the war
a far thunder—deserted
not deserting, home leave bought
by a blue coat stained deep red.

He crosses the boundary line
into Carolina, and soon
mountains pause, let land quick-fall
as light like a dawn breaks through,

reveals his cabin below,
his wife washing clothes, seen for
the first time in months, but when
he comes to Flynn Creek a door

shuts before him, the valley
slowly recedes, and he knows
what he is, knows he must leave
all of what's beloved, alone

but dips his hand in water
for a moment first, watches
it shape-shift like melted ice,
as his kneeling wife pauses,

wrists in flow, feels a known hand
brush her hand, looks up to see
his shade walking the ridge path
leading back to Tennessee.

THE PACT

Fog thick as cotton this dawn
five cousins sharing one name
meet at the mouth of Dismal,
Christmas gifts of brass-capped shells
bulging their pockets, bright knives
hip-worn like wallets, for one
a first shotgun the others
pass hand to hand, each truing
the sights with their clan's gray eyes
before given back and they
follow Laurel Fork deeper
into the gorge, boys who
share drinks from the same dipper
baling hay in July, share plugs
of tobacco as they top
rows of burley, but no chores
this late December morning,
free to hunt all day, but they
return at noon, the youngest
carried in their arms, his leg
a red explosion of bone,
the others wounded too, palms
slashed across lifelines, shared blood
shared again, a blood-oath made
so one alone will never
bear pity or blame, carried
the same way they will carry
the coffin, to the grave.

GOOD FRIDAY 2006:
SHELTON LAUREL

Below this knoll a man kneels.
Face close to the earth, he works
soil like a potter works clay,
kneading and shaping until
hands slowly open, reveal
a single green stalk before
he palms himself up the row
as if he hauls on his back
morning's sun-sprawl, a bringer
of light he cannot bring here
where oak trees knit tight shadows
across the marble that marks
the grave of David Shelton.
Thirteen years old, he had asked
one mercy, not to be shot
like his father—in the face.
He shares this grave with the others
hauled here through snow by women
to lie in Shelton ground. Wind lifts
green leaves, grows still. A man sows
his field the old way. The land
unscrolls like a palimpsest.

READING THE LEAVES

Across the creek, vines of fog
twine around poplar and ash,
distance dimming white, the world
grown close and older, and here
my uncle's work boots dirt-clogged
and dew-dark as he follows
the long sentence of each row,
pauses to thumb through damp leaves,
check close for blue mold, cutworm,
moving slow across a plot
of bottomland whose ending
is a barn, its tin roof spread
like a facedown book to hold
gold leaves of tobacco bound
to rafters, brittle pages
layered by time and weather,
strung together as Celts once
strung leaves on cords to compose
the first words of Albion.

BOY IN A BOXCAR

Smell of creosote, two rails,
knit by crossties, stitched across
the riverbank's brow, I sit
in the boxcar's wide, squared mouth,
legs dangling off, palms pressed flat,
watch from trapped dark the sun wake,
ignite a burnished flame on
the French Broad as water makes
a deeper track through Asheville,
hauls its cargo of bottles,
loosed planks and stick clots, all else
last night's thunder shook from banks.
Wheels underneath me break free
from years of rust, creak and turn,
westbound, Madison County's
higher mountains—the river
slowing, then still.

PENTECOST

Shingles flapped and scattered off
the roof like frightened chickens.
Rain didn't fall but slanted,
bruised stained glass to a purple
too dark for scripture, just hymns
sung from memory, sung soft
like whispers as I listened
to wind gusts sucking at nails,
planks shuddering, the steeple
creaking like a ship's masthead,
so closed my eyes, imagined
marble stones cast like anchors
behind the church over years
to hold those crossbeams upright
on that high wave of mountain.

WATAUGA COUNTY: 1962

Smell of honeysuckle bright
as dew beads stringing lines on
the writing spider's silk page,
night's cool lingering, the sun
awake but still lying down,
its slant-light seeping through gaps
of oak branches as the first
blackberry pings the milk pail's
emptiness, begins the slow
filling up, the plush feel of
berries only yesterday
red-green knots before steeped in
dark to a deep purple hue,
and as dawn passes, the pail
grows heavy, wearies my arm
until I sit down inside
that maze of briar I make
my kingdom, lift to my mouth
the sweet wine of blackberry,
my hands stained like royalty.

PRICE LAKE

In the shallows snake doctors
unknit the air with their green
and blue needles, but could not
free the line I'd got tangled so
I entered a grabble of briars,
tightroped the creekboard to where
my parents lay on a bank
softened by cove-moss, each turned
to the other, my mother's
hand tucked inside my father's
half-buttoned shirt, his fingers
brushing ground-lint from her hair,
and in that moment I knew
I never could belong there,
not in that moment, so slipped
away unnoticed, and though
the gift of that summer took
years to unveil, something stirred
even that day when they came
back to me, my mother's waist
cradled in my father's arm.

NEW POEMS

WET MOON

Come look, my grandmother said,
the moon's shed its skin, see how
big and bright, and when I asked
where the old skin was she laughed.
Later that night when I waked,
looked out the window, I found
moonglow draped on the barn roof
like clothes on a line, and wished
for a tall ladder to lean
against the wood slats and raise
a finger, brush the cool skin
that had once been cloaked with stars.

ACCENT

Theirs was not the coastal plain's
privileged plantation cadence,
more syllables spread like honey
over the tongue, much harsher
as if mountain air distilled
all but necessity from
their words, or was it winter
knocking chinks from cabin walls,
years breaking skin-flint dirt-rock,
isolate lives passed in cove
and hollow, always under
looming mountains, shadow-gloam
engulfing land like a lake,
hidden away until war
when they fought confederate
or federal, sometimes both,
their allegiances parlanced
by union of place and blood.

THE COUNTRY SINGER
EXPLAINS HER MUSE

Say you're on a bus between
Baton Rouge and New Orleans,
pills that got you through the show
slow to wear off, so you stare
out the window, searching for
darkened houses where you know
women sleep who live a life
you once lived, now sing about.
Let them dream as you write out
words and chords to find a song
made to get them through their day,
get you through a sleepless night
somewhere on a bus between
Baton Rouge and New Orleans.

WEASEL

Word-weave of mus and telos
(the Latin sobriquet) means
"mouse like a spear," and as if
to hone that point home one once
left its bleached skull in the throat
of an eagle, another
amazing the sky, alive
and sudden-winged, myth making
when a farmer watched it fall,
found the broad, flat reptile head
tearing free chunks of hawk-heart—
though any sighting is rare,
preferring their underworld,
navigating earthrivers
for mice and moles, surfacing
mostly at night, killing with
a fury of appetite.

TRACKS

Shift over, my father walks
the railroad tracks, on his back
the weight of his dreams—the books
he believes will take his life
beyond the weave room, so walks
crossties a mile, boards a bus
headed south fifty more miles,
lessons studied with what light
he can angle a page toward.
Three decades will pass before
he says, *it wasn't worth it,*
wish he had turned, headed back
down the tracks, back to the mill
he had led us away from.

MOODY SPRING

No family name but a flow
not counted on when a drought
lapped up what water might fill
a dipper or pail, given
a human nature, as though
the bestower believed such
vagary was another
sign of lost Eden, so now
too fallen to certain rise.

THE CALL

That afternoon as last light drained
from the hospital window,
he rose in the bed and called
not preacher, daughter or wife
but for his two black and tans,
as if they might keep at bay
what hovered in the shadows.
At that moment miles away
his hounds stirred, lifted their throats
and filled the mountain valley
with what near neighbors swore were
unearthly howls, ceased only
when the old man's last breath left,
and his dogs sprawled their bellies
against the earth and whimpered.

DIRECTION

Stay on the four-lane until
mountains sigh, make a valley
where off-ramps wait, only then
find that other way home, one
easy to miss (there's no sign).
Houses you pass are like beads
strung between trees and pasture,
most dark except some bare bulbs
blooming back porches yellow,
but what opens the heart's need
wide as this night are the rooms
lit as if someone waits up
to give direction should you
lose your way on this bypass
back to your knowable life.

Acknowledgments

Poems in this volume have appeared in the following venues:

"Last Service" in *Southwest Review*
"Under Jocassee" in *Carolina Quarterly*
"Taking Down the Lines" in *Poet Lore*
"Fall Creek" in *Passages North*
"Shee-Show" in *South Carolina Review*
"Deep Water" in *Mossy Creek Reader*
"In Dismal Gorge" in *Mossy Creek Reader*
"Black-Eyed Susans" in *Hiram Poetry Review*
"Whippoorwill" in *Raising the Dead*, Iris Press, 2002
"Shelton Laurel" in *Asheville Poetry Review*
"Wolf Laurel" in *Raising the Dead*, Iris Press, 2002
"Speckled Trout" in *Weber Studies*
"In the Barn" in *Weber Studies*
"Barn Burning: 1967" in *Chattahoochee Review*
"Work, for the Night Is Coming" in *Chattahoochee Review*
"The Debt" in *Southeast Review*
"Watauga County: 1974" in *Southeast Review*
"Burning the Field" in *Chattahoochee Review*
"At Reid Hartley's Junkyard" in *Tar River Poetry*
"Spear Point" in *Pembroke Magazine*
"Kephart in the Smokies" in *Greensboro Review*
"Barbed Wire" in *Quadrant* (Australia)

"The Search" in *Riverrun*

"Brightleaf" in *Atlanta Review*

"At Leicester Cemetery" in *North Carolina Literary Review*

"Madison County, June 1999" in *Raising the Dead*, Iris Press, 2002

"The Wolves in the Asheville Zoo" in *Raising the Dead*, Iris Press, 2002

"The Watch" in *Rattapallax*

"Bartram Leaves Jocassee" in *Raising the Dead*, Iris Press, 2002

"Carolina Parakeet" in *Sanctuary*

"The Vanquished" in *South Carolina Review*

"A Homestead on the Horsepasture" in *Chattahoochee Review*

"Bottomland" in *South Carolina Review*

"Tremor" in *South Carolina Review*

"Analepsis" in *American Literary Review*

"The Day the Gates Closed" in *Raising the Dead*, Iris Press, 2002

"Beyond the Dock" in *Raising the Dead*, Iris Press, 2002

"The Men Who Raised the Dead" in *Sewanee Review*

"On the Border" in *Cumberland Poetry Review*

"Plowing on Moonlight" in *Among the Believers*, Iris Press, 2002

"The Corpse Bird" in *Among the Believers*, Iris Press, 2002

"Madison County: 1864" in *Carolina Quarterly*

"On the Watauga" in *Among the Believers*, Iris Press, 2002

"Before" in *Among the Believers*, Iris Press, 2002

"The Exchange" in *Virginia Quarterly Review*

"A Preacher Who Takes Up Serpents Laments the Presence of Skeptics in His Church" in *Southern Review*

"The Afflicted" in *Among the Believers*, Iris Press, 2002

"The Preacher Is Called to Testify for the Accused" in *Now and Then*

"Signs" in *Among the Believers*, Iris Press, 2002

"Animal Hides" in *Southern Review*

"The Ascent" in *American Literary Review*

"From *The Mabinogion*" in *Among the Believers*, Iris Press, 2002

"In a Springhouse at Night" in *Mossy Creek Reader*

"Blue River" in *Mars Hill Literary Review*

"Spring Lizards" in *Among the Believers*, Iris Press, 2002

"Watershed" in *Now and Then*

"Ginseng" in *Prairie Schooner*

"Lasting Water" in *Prairie Schooner*

"Passage" in *Among the Believers*, Iris Press, 2002

"Barn Loft: 1959" in *Cumberland Poetry Review*

"The Fox" in *New England Review*

"August 1959: Morning Service" in *Virginia Quarterly Review*

"Abandoned Homestead in Watauga County" in *Texas Review*

"Among the Believers" in *Southern Review*

"Good Friday 1995, Driving Westward" in *Southern Review*

"Invocation" in *Eureka Mill*, Hub City, 1998

"Eureka" in *Southern Review*

"In a Dry Time" in *Eureka Mill*, Hub City, 1998

"Mill Village" in *Eureka Mill*, Hub City, 1998

"Low Water" in *DoubleTake*

"Spring Fever" in *Texas Review*

"Accident" in *New Virginia Review*

"The Sweeper" in *Eureka Mill*, Hub City, 1998

"The Famous Photographer Visits Eureka" in *Eureka Mill*, Hub City, 1998

"Bearings" in *Eureka Mill*, Hub City, 1998

"Jokes" in *Eureka Mill*, Hub City, 1998

"The Stretch-Out" in *Eureka Mill*, Hub City, 1998

"Flying Squadron" in *South Carolina Review*

"1934" in *South Carolina Review*

"Black and White" in *Eureka Mill*, Hub City, 1998

"Boundaries" in *Eureka Mill*, Hub City, 1998

"Revenant" in *Eureka Mill*, Hub City, 1998

"Brown Lung" in *Eureka Mill*, Hub City, 1998

"Plane Crash" in *Eureka Mill*, Hub City, 1998

"Listening to WBT" in *Poet Lore*

"Last Interview" in *Eureka Mill*, Hub City, 1998

"First Shift" in *Eureka Mill*, Hub City, 1998

"Photograph of My Parents Outside Eureka Cotton Mill. Dated June 1950" in *Dexter Review*

"July 1949" in *The Journal*

"First Memory" in *Wind*

"The Trout in the Springhouse" in *Quadrant* (Australia)

"Milking Traces" in *Quadrant* (Australia)

"Sleepwalking" in *Southern Poetry Review*

"Junk Car in Snow" in *Carolina Quarterly*

"Time Flow" in *Waking*, Hub City Press, 2011

"Watauga County: 1959" in *Carolina Quarterly*

"Bonding Fire" in *Waking*, Hub City Press, 2011

"Pocketknives" in *Oxford American*

"Shadetree" in *Southern Review*

"Car Tags" in *Waking*, Hub City Press, 2011

"Spillcorn" in *Waking*, Hub City Press, 2011

"Emrys" in *Sewanee Review*

"Mirror" in *Southern Review*

"Woman Among Lightning: Catawba County Fair, 1962" in *Southern Poetry Review*

"Bloodroot" in *Shenandoah*

"The Reaping" in *Sewanee Review*

"Elegy for Merle Watson" in *Shenandoah*

"White Wings" in *Shenandoah*

"Resonance" in *Waking*, Hub City Press, 2011

"Three A.M. and the Stars Were Out" in *Hudson Review*

"Genealogy" in *North Carolina Literary Review*

"The Code" in *Waking,* Hub City Press, 2011

"The Crossing" in *Shenandoah*

"The Pact" in *Gin Bender Review*

"Good Friday 2006: Shelton Laurel" in *Ploughshares*

"Reading the Leaves" in *Southern Review*

"Boy in a Boxcar" in *Sewanee Review*

"Pentecost" in *Iron Mountain Review*

"Watauga County: 1962" in *Appalachian Journal*

"Price Lake" in *Cortland Review*

"Accent" in *Atlanta Review*

"Moody Spring" in *Atlantic Review*